really
RUDe
RhYMES

Also edited by John Foster

A Century of Children's Poems
101 Favourite Poems

Loopy Limericks
Ridiculous Rhymes
Dead Funny
Teasing Tongue-Twisters
Completely Crazy Poems
Seriously Scary Poems
Fiendishly Funny Poems

# really RUDE RhYMES

picked by John Foster

Illustrated by Nathan Reed

HarperCollins *Children's Books*

First published by HarperCollins *Children's Books* in 2004
HarperCollins *Children's Books* is an imprint of HarperCollins*Publishers* Ltd,
77-85 Fulham Palace Road, Hammersmith, W6 8JB

The HarperCollins *Children's Books* website is
www.harpercollinschildrensbooks.co.uk

1 3 5 7 9 8 6 4 2

This edition copyright © John Foster 2004
Illustrations by Nathan Reed 2004
The acknowledgements on page 96
constitute an extension of this copyright page.

ISBN 0 00 714804 6

The authors, illustrator and editor assert the moral right to
be identified as the authors, illustrator and editor of this work.

Printed and bound in England by
Clays Ltd, St Ives plc

Conditions of Sale

# Contents

## Bottom Lines

| | | |
|---|---|---|
| If I Lost My Trousers | Rony Robinson | 8 |
| Just Watch | John Kitching | 8 |
| Kiltie, Kiltie | John Rice | 9 |
| The Three-Letter Word | Cynthia Rider | 10 |
| Wear Something White at Night | Brenda Williams | 12 |
| A Cheeky Boy | Marian Swinger | 14 |
| A Pain in the Bum | Ivor Cheek | 16 |
| The Bottom Line | Trevor Harvey | 18 |
| Hot Cross Bum | John Kitching | 18 |

## Naughty Nonsense

| | | |
|---|---|---|
| Mary Had | Colin Macfarlane | 20 |
| Little Jack Horner | Simon Byrne | 22 |
| Hey Diddle Diddle | Simon Byrne | 22 |
| This Little Dog | Tim Hopkins | 23 |
| Mary, Mary, Quite Contrary | Ivor Cheek | 24 |
| Scowling Billy | Ivor Cheek | 24 |
| Jack's Complaint | Simon Byrne | 25 |
| There Was a Young Farmer Called Max | Anon | 26 |
| Did You Hear About... | John Foster | 28 |
| Mary Had a Little Bear | Anon | 30 |

## Noxious Noises and Odious Odours

| | | |
|---|---|---|
| Phew! | Marcus Parry | 32 |
| Silence in School! | Penny Dolan | 34 |
| A Downward Course | Anon | 35 |
| Beans | Anon | 36 |
| Beans on Toast | Marian Swinger | 37 |
| A Poem About the Dangers of Swallowing Dubblegum | Paul Cookson | 38 |
| Silent But Deadly | Granville Lawson | 40 |
| A Laddie Called Alistair Crumb | Marian Swinger | 42 |
| A Student from Sparta | Anon | 43 |
| Speeding Down the Motorway | Anon | 44 |
| A Schoolboy Let Off, With a Boom | Marian Swinger | 46 |
| Own Up | Lindsay MacRae | 48 |

## Knicker Snickers

| | | |
|---|---|---|
| Knickers! | John Coldwell | 50 |
| Esmerelda's Knickers | Brenda Williams | 52 |
| I Am a Girl Guide Dressed in Blue | Anon | 54 |

When Grandma Sat on a Staple    John Foster    56
A Naughty Girl Called Flo    Anon    56
A Certain Young Lady Named Lily    Anon    57
Bloomers    Debjani Chatterjee    58
Nicola Nicholas    John Foster    58

## JUNGLE SMELLS

Jungle Smells, Jungle Smells    John Rice    60
Baboons' Bottoms    Coral Rumble    62
A Bug and a Flea    Anon    64
Under the Apple Tree    Anon    65
The Black Cat and the White Cat    Anon    66
Our Cat    Mike Johnson
   and Helen Mason    67
My Dog's Nose    Colin Macfarlane    68
A Question of Dogs    Aislinn
   and Larry O'Loughlin    69
A Worse Alternative    Michael Dugan    70

## CAUGHT SHORTS

Caught Short    Graham Shaw    72
Urgent Request    John Foster    72
Diary of a Toilet Seat    Daniel Phelps    73
Manners    Anon    74
St Bride    Barbara Moore    75
Here's a Wee Problem...    Trevor Harvey    76
D is for Diarrhoea    Jean Ure    77
Old King Cole and Farmer White    Anon    78
A Sticky Situation    Ivor Cheek    80
There Was an Old Man of Peru    Marian Swinger    81
You're in Trouble    John Kitching    82

## NAKED TRUTHS

The Naked Truth    Mike Johnson    84
W Stands for Willy    Jean Ure    86
Newsflash!    Granville Lawson    86
Ask No Questions    Ivor Cheek    87
Belt Up!    Granville Lawson    88
The End of Term    John Coldwell    89
Steven Bunn    Granville Lawson    90
There Was a Young Bather from Bewes    Anon    92
There Once Was a Lady of Erskine    Anon    94
There Was a Young Fellow Called Jude    Ivor Cheek    94
Epitaph    Wes Magee    95

Acknowledgements    96

# Bottom Lines

# If I Lost My Trousers

If I lost my trousers,
Tell you what I'd do.
Paint a face upon my bum
And come and smile at you.

Rony Robinson

# Just Watch

See my finger.
See my thumb.
See my tattoo
On my bum.

Watch my cheeks
As I make them wiggle.
Watch my tattoo.
See it wriggle.

John Kitching

# Kiltie, Kiltie

I come from a land
full of little Scotties.
We all wear kilts
and have freezing botties!

John Rice

# The Three-Letter Word

Oh, the three-letter word,

The three-letter word,

The one that rhymes with 'rum',

Is one of those words,

Those wonderful words

That can stop you feeling glum.

It's a plum of a word

The three-letter word,

It's not in the least humdrum.

You can sing it and hum it

And shout it on summits

And whisper it to your chum.

Oh, it's such a good word

The three-letter word,

It's a word you must have heard.

And if I could spell it

I'd certainly tell it,

But I can't — which is rather absurd.

But it's part of your body

(Though not your thumb)

And on a hard seat

It can go quite numb.

Oh, it's one of those words

That *is* glorious fun,

The three-letter word

That rhymes with 'rum'.

Cynthia Rider

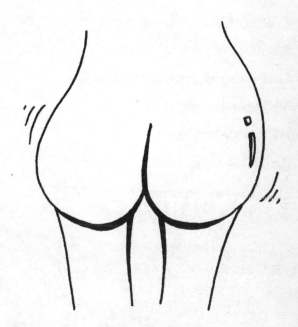

# Wear Something White at Night

Alexander Alan Mumm
Had a white and shiny bum.
When walking out
One dark bleak night
He used his bottom
As a light.

And so the drivers
Passing by
Saw a moon, not in the sky
But near the ground
Along the track
And just beneath his anorak!

## Brenda Williams

# A Cheeky Boy

A cheeky boy called Peter Prune,
at every chance he got, would moon.
His teacher, Miss Matilda Peake
would glimpse his great round bum and shriek
and a cycling vicar made a fuss
as, gleaming from a passing bus,
it waggled rudely through the gloom.
Then in the doctor's waiting room,
it left poor spinster, Ada Black,
prostrated with a heart attack,
and on the recreation ground,

the awful boy was often found

mooning high upon the slide

attracting notice far and wide,

until the day he bared his all,

bottom bouncing like a ball

and old Joe Bloggs, short sighted soul,

kicked it hard and shouted, 'Goal!'

It gave the boy a dreadful scare

and running, clutching at his rear,

a hobnailed boot print on his bum,

he hastened, howling, home to Mum

while people yelled in jubilation

at Peter Prune's humiliation.

Marian Swinger

# A Pain in the Bum

Lavender Lottum
Has an itchy bottom.

Jeremy Styles
Has painful piles.

Theobald Thrum
Has a boil on his bum.

Dorothy Deer
Has severe diarrhoea.

Hermione Hants
Has ants in her pants.

Norman Nation
Has constipation.

Verity Flickers
Has a wasp in her knickers

And Percival Parting
Cannot stop...

Ivor Cheek

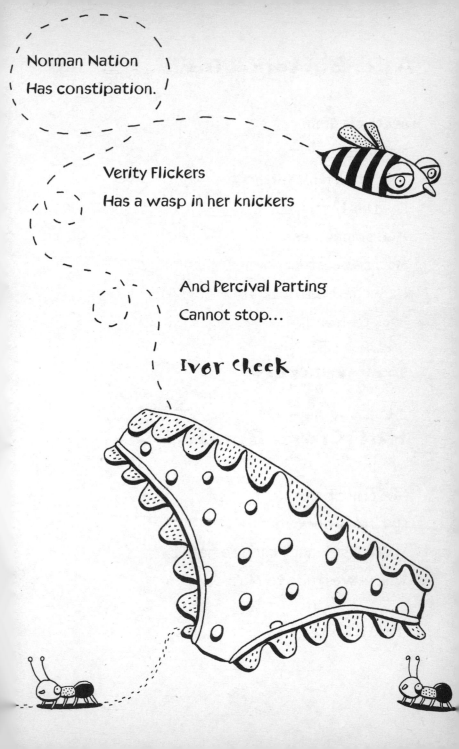

# The Bottom Line

My Uncle Ernie
Has a tum
That sticks out further
Than his bum;
And sometimes,
As a comic stunt,
He wears his trousers
Back-to-front!

Trevor Harvey

# Hot Cross Bum!

Hot cross bum!
Hot cross bum!
That's just what I used to get
When I was rude to Mum!

John Kitching

# Naughty Nonsense

# Mary Had

Mary had a little lamb,
at first she called it Sindy.
She fed it beans three times a day
and changed its name to Windy!

Mary had a little goat,
at first she called it Lily,
but when she took a closer look
she changed its name to Billy.

Mary had a little lamb,
its fleece was white as snow,
and everywhere that Mary went,
the lamb was sure to go.

She took it to her school
but in the middle of a sum
it skipped across the room
and bit her teacher on the bum!

**Colin Macfarlane**

# Little Jack Horner

Little Jack Horner
sat in his corner
pushing his bum cheeks high.
He gave a quick squeeze
held on to his knees
and farted his way up to the sky.

Simon Byrne

# Hey Diddle Diddle

Hey diddle diddle
the cat had a piddle
all over the kitchen floor
the little dog laughed
to see such fun
so the cat did a little bit more.

Simon Byrne

# This Little Dog

This little dog was a barker,
This little dog gnawed a bone,
And this little dog liked to wee wee wee
On a lamppost near his home.

Tim Hopkins

no dogs
weeing!

# Mary, Mary, Quite Contrary

Mary, Mary, quite contrary,
Why are you looking so glum?
I went for a pee behind the hedge
And a nettle stung my bum.

Ivor Cheek


# Scowling Billy

There he goes
Scowling Billy.
Fell on some thistles
And pricked his willy.

Ivor Cheek

# Jack's Complaint

Why should I be nimble?

Why should I be quick?

Why am I jumping over a candlestick?

    I'm not very happy.

    I'm very, very glum.

Have you see the burn marks on the

    back of my bum?

I don't want to jump for the rest of time.

I want to get out of this nursery rhyme.

**Simon Byrne**

# There Was a Young Farmer Called Max

There was a young farmer called Max
Who avoided paying petrol tax.
It was simple you see,
For his tractor burned pee
From his grandfather's herd of tame yaks.

Anon

# Did You Hear About...

Did you hear about
My auntie Nellie?
She's got a pimple
On her belly.

Did you hear about
My uncle John?
He went to work
With no trousers on.

Did you hear about
My auntie Prue?
She spent all week
Locked in the loo.

Did you hear about
My cousin Dottie?
She got her head
Stuck in her potty.

Did you hear about
My uncle Jude?
He rode his bicycle
In the nude.

Did you hear about
My uncle's chum?
He got a blister
On the cheek of his bum.

**John Foster**

# Mary Had a Little Bear

Mary had a little bear,

To which she was so kind

That everywhere that Mary went

You saw her bear behind.

Anon

# Noxious Noises and Odious Odours

# Phew!

Some people call them Windy Pops,
To others they are Fluffs.
Or Trouser Coughs or Botty Burps
Or Poots or Grunts or Guffs.

Some people talk of Rotten Eggs,
Or Early Morning Thunder,
Or Cheesy Toasties, Flutterbasts,
Kabooms or Whootzie Wonders.

There's SBD's and SBV's,
Putt-putts and Smelly Jelly.
Taco Torpedos, Talking Pants,
Ham Slams and Bubbling Belly.

Toot-toots and Gassers, Back Door Blasts
And Brown Air Biscuits too.
Cheek Slappers, Butzers, Flappers, Pips,
Fizz Fuzz and Whiffy Woo.

But though they try to hide them,
Or think up these fancy names,
Whatever people call their farts
The smell still stays the same.

Marcus Parry

guffff!

rt!

# Silence in School!

Oh, I am the ghost of the gurgles! I haunt each
  silent space.
Whenever the school is quiet, I long to fill the
  place
With gargling grumbling tummies, with sudden
  burps and coughs
With loud rude-bottom noises and smelly
  blowing-offs
Oh, I am the ghost of the gurgles, and I sneak the
  school along –
You will know I'm here by the sound you fear –
And my ghost-of-the-gurgle pong!

**Penny Dolan**

# A Downward Course

A sigh is but a breath of air
That issues from the heart,
But when it takes a downward course
It's simply called a fart.

Anon

# Beans

Baked beans are good for your heart
The more you eat the more you fart
The more you fart the better you feel
Baked beans with every meal!

Anon

# Beans on Toast

Amelia loved beans on toast
and so did sister Susie,
but beans were banned the day their bath
became a giant Jacuzzi.

Marian Swinger

38

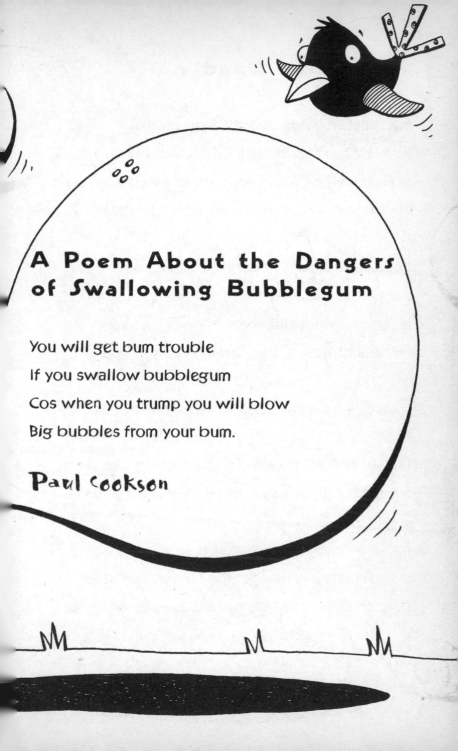

# A Poem About the Dangers of Swallowing Bubblegum

You will get bum trouble

If you swallow bubblegum

Cos when you trump you will blow

Big bubbles from your bum.

Paul Cookson

# Silent But Deadly

My silent but deadly is licensed to kill
You'd better stand back or it probably will.
I can tell when your faces are screwed up in pain
My silent but deadly has struck once again!

Deep in my bowels a storm is amassing
And somebody's in for a terrible gassing.
It's such a great pity I've only just met you
My silent but deadly is coming to get you!

It creeps from my trousers when nobody knows
Invisibly getting up everyone's nose.
I know when you're wriggling and writhing like snakes
My silent but deadly's still got what it takes!

It's savage, it's lethal, breathe in if you dare
A well rotted cabbage just cannot compare.
I watch as your face turns a deep shade of grey
My silent but deadly has blown you away!

This noiseless assassin will pay you a call
And knock you unconscious in no time at all.
As though you've been hit by a truckload of bricks
My silent but deadly just knocked you for six!

You were born to receive I was born to despatch
And whatever the reason do not strike a match.
I'll know when I see you collapse in a heap
My silent but deadly has put you to sleep!

You don't know who did it, you haven't a clue
Someone is guilty but you don't know who.
For the great thing about my untraceable bomb
You know where it went but you don't know
    where it's from!

**Granville Lawson**

# A Laddie Called Alistair Crumb

A laddie called Alistair Crumb

could play a cool tune with his bum.

He'd mastered the art

of fine tuning the fart

while accompanying himself on the drum.

Marian Swinger

# A Student from Sparta

A musical student from Sparta

Was a truly magnificent farter;

On the strength of one bean

He'd fart 'God Save the Queen',

And Beethoven's 'Moonlight Sonata'.

Anon

# Speeding Down
# the Motorway

Speeding down the motorway

At a hundred and four

My dad did a big one

And blew off the door!

The engine couldn't take it

The bonnet blew apart

And all because my dad did

A supersonic fart!

Anon

# A Schoolboy Let Off, with a Boom

A schoolboy let off, with a boom,
a fart like the last trump of doom.
His teacher walked past
and was caught in the blast
and blown right out of the room.

**Marian Swinger**

# Own Up

Who expostulated lately?

Who crawled out of their shell?

Who let a ripper

Which stinks like a kipper

Out of the jaws of hell?

Who squeezed a sneaker?

Who leaked a leaker?

Who's looking guilty as well?

Someone please own up

Behave like a grown-up.

Who made that horrible smell?

Lindsay MacRae

# Knicker Snickers

# Knickers!

Patti Coomber's in her nan's winter bloomers

Angela Carruthers has borrowed her brother's

Dot Cleese – has knickers that cover her knees

Lucy Caper has pants made of paper

Harriet Hawkes is in boxer shorts

Her best friend, Jilly, likes pants pink and frilly

Susie Dorson has her leather drawers on

Stacey Casey likes her undies lacy

Samantha Vickers tucks her skirt in her knickers

And Julie Dredd wears hers on her head

But as for the knickers of Clarice Bean

She wears trousers – so they've never been seen

John Coldwell

# Esmerelda's Knickers

Esmerelda Phoebe Flickers
Bought herself gigantic knickers.

The reason why she went and got 'em
Was to cover her enormous bottom

But when she found they didn't fit her
She sold them to the local vicar.

Now he too had a large posterior
Though by comparison, it was inferior.

So whilst they almost served his purpose,
They drooped below his Sunday surplice.

His congregation got the titters
To see him in his frilly knickers

And so one day after the sermon
He sold his knickers to an airman.

The airman thought them really cute
And used them as a parachute!

Brenda Williams

# I Am a Girl Guide Dressed in Blue

I am a girl guide dressed in blue,
These are the actions I can do –
Salute to the captain,
Curtsy to the queen,
Show my panties to the football team.

Anon

# When Grandma Sat on a Staple

When Grandma sat on a staple,
She shot in the air with a shriek.
Where her knickers were thin,
It pierced the skin
And left a blue bruise on her cheek.

John Foster

# A Naughty Girl Called Flo

A naughty girl called Flo
Wanted her knickers to show.
So she wore a skirt
As short as a shirt
And kept on bending down low.

Anon

# A Certain Young Lady Named Lily

A certain young lady named Lily

Likes knickers – light pink and frilly.

In winter she wears

Maybe three or four pairs

Which stops her bum feeling too chilly.

Anon

# Bloomers

Sometimes it's fun to look at clothes
and try to guess what inspired those –
their fantastic shapes and colours.
But I'm sure that our school bloomers,
which the nuns recommend for gym,
in starchy cotton, rough and grim,
a one-size brilliant maroon
and baggy like a twin balloon,
were made by designers who saw
a monkey's bottom – red and raw.

Debjani Chatterjee


# Nicola Nicholas

Nicola Nicholas couldn't care less.
Nicola Nicholas tore her dress.
Nicola Nicholas tore her knickers.
Now Nicola Nicholas is knickerless.

John Foster

# Jungle smells

# Jungle Smells, Jungle Smells

Jungle smells, jungle smells
sing a song well sung,
when you trample through the trees
you might step on some dung.

Oh jungle smells, jungle smells
no one bothers with a loo,
for all the creatures hereabouts
don't care where they do a poo.

Oh jungle smells, jungle smells
you'll hear the sound of sloppings,
so careful where you sit my friend,
watch out for monkey droppings!

John Rice

# Baboons' Bottoms

Baboons' bottoms
Are so rude,
Red and shiny
And so nude;
Lumpy, bumpy,
With a laugh
They flash them
For each photograph!

Baboons' bottoms,
Bright and lewd,
Blue and yucky,
Oh so crude!
I think my aunt
Would be more happy
If they were made
To wear a nappy!

Baboons' bottoms,
What a sight!
Designed to give
Your gran a fright;
Who can't believe
The age-old rumour
That God has got
A sense of humour.

Coral Rumble

# A Bug and a Flea

A bug and a flea went out to sea
Upon a reel of cotton;
The flea was drowned but the bug was found
Stuck to a mermaid's bottom.

Anon

a flea?

# Under the Apple Tree

As I sat under the apple tree,

A birdie sent his love to me,

And as I wiped it from my eye,

I said, 'Thank goodness cows can't fly.'

Anon

# The Black Cat and the White Cat

Oh! The black cat piddled in the white cat's eye.

The white cat said, 'Cor blimey!'

'I'm sorry, sir, I piddled in your eye.

I didn't know you was behind me.'

**Anon**

# Our Cat

Our cat has diarrhoea,
and I think she's really clever.
She missed hitting me completely,
it all landed on our Trevor.

Mike Johnson and Helen Mason

## My Dog's Nose

My dog has a lovely, rubbery nose
but I can't help but worry over where it goes:
it snuffs around lampposts and, on meeting a friend,
it sniffs the other's nose... then the opposite end!

Colin Macfarlane

# A Question of Dogs

If dachshunds dashed
and boxers boxed
and bulldogs all went 'moo'
and wolfhounds howled
and sheepdogs baaed
what would shih-tzus do?

**Aislinn and Larry O'Loughlin**

# A Worse Alternative

The dogs that walk along our street
leave little gifts that don't smell sweet,
requiring me so often to
take off and carefully scrape my shoe.
Mind you, it's really worse, I swear,
to step on one while feet are bare.

Michael Dugan

# caught Shorts

# Caught Short

I am sitting on the toilet
And I've just done a poo
But I can't see any toilet roll
And I don't know what to do!

Graham Shaw


# Urgent Request

When Mustapha Krapp met Wanda Piddle
They didn't say, 'How do you do?'
Instead they said, 'Excuse me,
Where's the nearest loo?'

John Foster

# Diary of a Toilet Seat

Today's been an up and down kind of day
A girl then boy kind of day
A sunny and showers kind of day
Not a sit down on the job kind of day
BUTT a stand up – sit down kind of day
A meeting up with old friends kind of day
And lots of new faces kind of day.

I hope tonight is a lie down and sleep kind of night
BUTT I bet it will be another
Stand up and guard the tank kind of night.

No BUTTS they say... no BUTTS
If only that were true.

**Daniel Phelps**

# Manners

If you sprinkle
When you winkle
Please be neat
And wipe the seat.

Anon

# St Bride

An unfortunate man from St Bride
Fell in the urinal and died;
The next day his brother
Fell into another:
Now they're Resting in Pees side by side.

Barbara Moore

# Here's a Wee Problem...

Before you cook those vegetables,
I think they'll need re-straining...
You left the pan without its lid
And my brother's potty training.

Trevor Harvey

# D is for Diarrhoea

D is for Diarrhoea

Also known as THE RUNS.

It comes from fear

Or upset tums.

It is gross and mucky.

Decidedly yucky.

Jean Ure

# Old King Cole and Farmer White

Old King Cole was a merry old soul
A merry old soul was he
He called for a light in the middle of the night
To go to the WC.

The WC was occupied
And so was the bathroom sink
But it has to be done
Oh it had to be done
So out of the window it went.

Now Farmer White was passing by
And heard a rumble in the sky
So he looked up as it came down
And now they call him Farmer Brown.

Anon

# A Sticky Situation

There was a young fellow called Stu
Who dreamed he had swallowed some glue.
He woke up feeling gummy
With a pain in his tummy,
Sat down and got stuck to the loo!

Ivor Cheek

# There Was an Old Man of Peru

There was an old man of Peru

who spent forty-four days on the loo.

'Well, I've eaten a bed

and eight armchairs,' he said.

'And they're taking some time to pass through.'

Marian Swinger

# You're in Trouble

'If we adopt the euro,'
I said to my best mate,
'We'll never spend a penny:
We'll have to euronate!'

John Kitching

# Naked Truths

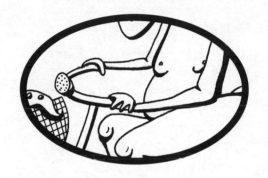

# The Naked Truth

Last summer, on a secret beach —
I went there, with my dad and mum —
I heard a nudist humming this:
'Bum, titty, bum, titty, bum, bum, bum.'

The weather wasn't very warm,
I think his bottom had gone numb.
In just his shoes, he had the blues,
'Bum, titty, bum, titty, bum, bum, bum.'

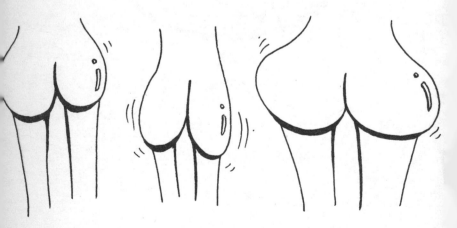

He scratched his head, he scratched his arm,

he scratched his shoulders and his tum:

without a stitch, things often itch.

'Bum, titty, bum, titty, bum, bum, bum.'

He said, 'Games are odd, with nothing on,

Especially a rugby scrum

And volleyball's strangest of all.

Bum, titty, bum, titty, bum, bum, bum.'

'Bum, titty, bum, titty, bum, bum, bum.'

Mike Johnson

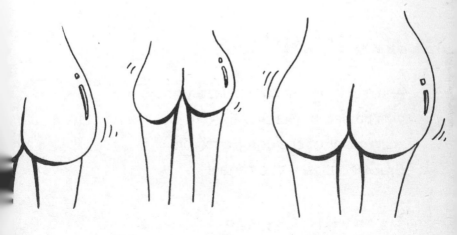

85

# W Stands for Willy

W stands for willy,
Both childish and silly.
There's another word, so I have heard,
Which is really quite a riddle.
In the U. S. of A., or so they say,
When people want to piddle,
Their Johnson is the thing they use.
A bit of a strange word to choose.
Poor old Johnson! Who was he?
Now he's as rude as rude can be.

Jean Ure


# Newsflash!

A streaker in the church last night
Was named as Gerald Morgan.
A member of the congregation
Grabbed him by the organ!

Granville Lawson

# Ask No Questions

Ask no questions
Hear no lies
Our teacher's forgotten
To do up his flies!

Don't you look.
Don't you stare.
Teacher's wearing
Blue underwear

Ivor Cheek

# Belt Up!

An embarrassed young teacher called Brown
Packed his bags, sold his house and left town.
For in lessons that morning
Without any warning
His trousers and Y-fronts fell down!

Granville Lawson

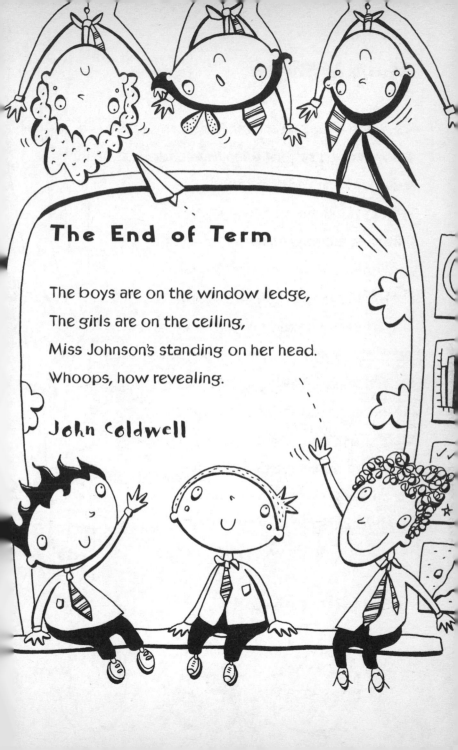

# The End of Term

The boys are on the window ledge,
The girls are on the ceiling,
Miss Johnson's standing on her head.
Whoops, how revealing.

John Coldwell

# Steven Bunn

Have you heard of Steven Bunn

Who went to school with flies undone.

Amazingly he did not know

But Steven Bunn was flying low.

Chirpy as a circus clown

And unaware his zip was down!

People laughed when he walked by

But Steven Bunn did not know why.

Assembly came – surprise, surprise

Steven Bunn has won a prize.

He marched out front – a thousand eyes

Were glued to Steven's gaping flies.

He stood up there for all to see

I thank the Lord it wasn't me.

I bet you're glad it wasn't you

– His underpants were missing too!

## Granville Lawson

# There Was a Young Bather from Bewes

There was a young bather from Bewes
Who lay on the banks of the Ouse.
His radio blared
And passers-by stared
For all he had on was the news.

Anon

# There Once Was a Lady of Erskine

There once was a lady of Erskine
Who had remarkably fair skin.
When I said to her, 'Mabel,
You look best in sable,'
She replied, 'I look best in my bearskin.'

Anon

# There Was a Young Fellow Called Jude

There was a young fellow called Jude
Who swam in the sea in the nude.
But he got such a fright
When a fish took a bite
Of a 'worm' he mistook for some food!

Ivor Cheek

# Epitaph

Here lies
Acker Abercrombie,
crazy name,
crazy zombie.
Slightly scary,
rather rude,
he walks at midnight
in the nude.

Wes Magee

# Acknowledgements

We are grateful to the following authors for permission to include the following poems, all of which are published for the first time in this collection:

Simon Byrne: 'Little Jack Horner', 'Hey Diddle Diddle' and 'Jack's Complaint' all copyright © Simon Byrne 2004. Debjani Chatterjee: 'Bloomers' copyright © Debjani Chatterjee 2004. Ivor Cheek: 'A Pain in the Bum', 'Mary, Mary, Quite Contrary', 'Scowling Billy', 'A Sticky Situation', 'Ask No Questions' and 'There Was a Young Fellow Called Jude' all copyright © John Foster 2004. John Coldwell: 'Knickers!' and 'The End of Term' both copyright © John Coldwell 2004. Paul Cookson: 'A Poem About the Dangers of Swallowing Bubblegum' copyright © Paul Cookson 2004. Penny Dolan: 'Silence in School' copyright © Penny Dolan 2004. Michael Dugan: 'A Worse Alternative' copyright © Michael Dugan 2004. John Foster: 'Did You Hear About…', 'When Grandma Sat on a Staple' and 'Urgent Request' all copyright © John Foster 2004. Trevor Harvey: 'The Bottom Line' and 'Here's a Wee Problem' both copyright © Trevor Harvey 2004. Tim Hopkins: 'This Little Dog' copyright © Tim Hopkins 2004. Mike Johnson: 'The Naked Truth' copyright © Mike Johnson 2004. Mike Johnson and Helen Mason: 'Our Cat' copyright © Mike Johnson and Helen Mason 2004. John Kitching: 'Just Watch', 'Hot Cross Bum' and 'You're in Trouble' all copyright © John Kitching 2004. Granville Lawson: 'Silent But Deadly', 'Newsflash!', 'Belt Up!' and 'Steven Bunn' all copyright © Granville Lawson 2004. Colin Macfarlane: 'Mary Had' and 'My Dog's Nose' both copyright © Colin Macfarlane 2004. Lindsay MacRae: 'Own Up' copyright © Lindsay MacRae 2004. Wes Magee: 'Epitaph' copyright © Wes Magee 2004. Barbara Moore: 'St Bride' copyright © Barbara Moore 2004. Marcus Parry: 'Phew!' copyright © Marcus Parry 2004. Daniel Phelps: 'Diary of a Toilet Seat' copyright © Daniel Phelps 2004. John Rice: 'Kiltie, Kiltie' and 'Jungle Smells, Jungle Smells' both copyright © John Rice 2004. Cynthia Rider: 'The Three-Letter Word' copyright © Cynthia Rider 2004. Rony Robinson: 'If I Lost My Trousers' copyright © Rony Robinson 2004. Coral Rumble: 'Baboons' Bottoms' copyright © Coral Rumble 2004. Graham Shaw: 'Caught Short' copyright © Graham Shaw 2004. Marian Swinger: 'Beans on Toast', 'A Schoolboy Let Off, With a Boom', 'A Laddie Called Alistair Crumb', 'There Was an Old Man of Peru' and 'A Cheeky Boy' all copyright © Marian Swinger 2004. Brenda Williams: 'Wear Something White at Night' and 'Esmeralda's Knickers' both copyright © Brenda Williams 2004.

We also acknowledge permission to include previously published poems:

John Foster: 'Nicola Nicholas' copyright © John Foster 2000 from *Climb Aboard the Poetry Plane* (Oxford University Press), included by permission of the author. Aislinn and Larry O'Loughlin: 'A Question of Dogs' copyright © Aislinn and Larry O'Loughlin from *Worms Can't Fly* published by Wolfhound Press (An imprint of Merlin Publishing). Jean Ure: 'D is for Diarrhoea' and 'W Stands for Willy' copyright © Jean Ure 2000. Extracted from *The Secret Life of Sally Tomato* and reproduced by kind permission of the publishers, HarperCollins.